Dear Kailyn, create your world!

-DADDY

Today! Today! Today is the day!
I get to see my daddy! Hooray!
It's his weekend, and he never forgets! That's why my daddy is just the best!

He does all the things a mommy can do! He's so big and strong and knows Kung fu.

He always says, "Dream big, daughter, create your world! Let them see your power, girl! And if they don't. It's ok! Some shine too bright for minds at bay."

Even at night, we *gaze* upon stars. Lay in the grass and speak about Mars. We talk of the future, and what may become, then we speak of the *ancestors* and where we are from.

Royalty! *Legacy*! Science! And medicine! *Innovate* and create! It's never too late! *Discover* your mind. A tool or weapon? Princess! Please use *discretion*!

Use your gifts to *discover* yourself. Take the time to *train* your mind. Listen to the sounds, the smell, the feel! Breathe! It's your mind; use that to see! Not just your eyes!

We create memories when we sing and dance. We watch movies and eat snacks. I ride on his back. And just when I've thought we've laughed too much, my dad falls asleep; he snores a bunch!

When the weekend is over, we say goodbye! But try to stay *tough*, so that we don't cry. And if we do, we promise to smile. Being sad too long just isn't our *style*.

The End

... Until next week!

GLOSSARY

Ancestor: A person in your family that lived a long time before you were born

Discover: To find (something or someone) before anyone else

Discretion: The freedom or authority to use one's own judgment

Gaze: To look steadily; stare

Innovate: To carry out a new idea, approach, or method

Legacy: Anything that is passed down from your ancestors; or someone who came before

Royalty: A member of a royal family; the power or position of a royal person

Style: The manner in which something is said or done

Tough: Hard to break; strong

Train: To teach skills or actions

Made in United States
North Haven, CT
29 June 2022

20797891R00015